Caring for Your
Hedgehog

Nancy Mulder

Weigl Publishers Inc.

Editor
Heather C. Hudak

Design
Warren Clark

Published by Weigl Publishers Inc.
350 5th Avenue, Suite 3304, PMB 6G
New York, NY 10118-0069
Web site: www.weigl.com

Library of Congress Cataloging-in-Publication Data

Mulder, Nancy.
  Caring for your hedgehog / Nancy Mulder.
     p. cm. -- (Caring for your pet)
  Includes index.
  ISBN 1-59036-470-8 (library binding : alk. paper) -- ISBN 1-59036-471-6 (softcover : alk. paper)
  1. Hedgehogs as pets--Juvenile literature. I. Title. II. Series: Caring for your pet (Mankato, Minn.)
  SF459.H43M85 2007
  636.933'2--dc22

2006016107

Printed in the United States of America
1 2 3 4 5 6 7 8 9 0 10 09 08 07 06

Locate the hedgehog paw prints throughout the book to find useful tips on caring for your pet.

Photograph and Text Credits
Every reasonable effort has been made to trace ownership and to obtain permission to reprint copyright material. The publishers would be pleased to have any errors or omissions brought to their attention so that they may be corrected in subsequent printings.

Cover: Hedgehogs are considered "pocket pets" because they are cute, friendly, and small enough to fit inside a shirt or jacket pocket.

All of the Internet URLs given in the book were valid at the time of publication. However, due to the dynamic nature of the Internet, some addresses may have changed, or sites may have ceased to exist since publication. While the author and publisher regret any inconvenience this may cause readers, no responsibility for any such changes can be accepted by either the author or the publisher.

Contents

Prickly Pals

A hedgehog covered with sharp spines, or quills, is not the cuddliest animal. Once you get to know one, though, it can be a friendly pet. Each one of these curious little creatures has a different personality. Hedgehog owners are provided with hours of fun and entertainment as they watch their pet explore inside his cage. It is also fun to watch a hedgehog run on an exercise wheel or climb around his surroundings.

If you must pick up a hedgehog, you can use a large slotted spoon to prevent being pricked by his quills.

■ Hedgehogs feel like the bristles of a hairbrush.

While hedgehogs are small and easy to care for, they are still a big responsibility for a pet owner. You must care for your pet for his entire life. The hedgehog will need daily feeding, exercise, attention, and love. His cage, toys, and food and water containers should be cleaned often. If he becomes ill, you may need to take the hedgehog to a **veterinarian**. Be sure you are able to spend the time and money a pet hedgehog requires before buying one. It is important to know that when a hedgehog feels scared he will curl up in a tight ball with his quills showing. If you try handling a scared hedgehog, you might be pricked by his quills. Learning about hedgehogs is an important part of making a healthy home for your new pet.

■ Hedgehogs curl up in a ball to protect the parts of their body that are not covered with quills.

Fascinating Facts

- Albino hedgehogs have white quills, pink skin, and red eyes. They are born without the special dyes, called pigments, that given them color.
- Moonrats from southeast Asia are related to hedgehogs. They look like hedgehogs with no quills.

Pet Profiles

There are 15 **species** of hedgehogs. Most pet hedgehogs in North America are African pygmy hedgehogs. The African pygmy hedgehog is also known as the four-toed hedgehog. In the wild, hedgehogs only live for 2 to 3 years. Pet hedgehogs have been known to live to 8 to 10 years of age.

FOUR-TOED

- Is also know as the African pygmy hedgehog
- Quills are brown or gray with cream tips
- Face and stomach are white
- Has a very short tail
- May travel across several miles in one night

ALGERIAN

- One of the smaller species of hedgehog; only 8 to 10 inches (20 to 25 centimeters) long
- At the crown of its head it has no quills
- Does not hibernate in winter
- Paler in color than most hedgehogs

SOUTH AFRICAN

- Small, white spines with black band around the tips
- Face, limbs, and tail are covered with brown hair
- A white band across the forehead sometimes extends over the shoulders
- Long legs
- Mostly **nocturnal**, but may be active in the day if the weather is cool

Since hedgehogs are native to warm climates, such as desert areas in Africa, they prefer temperatures between 75 and 85° Fahrenheit (24 to 29° Celsius). When temperatures dip too low, hedgehogs go into winter **hibernation**. In nature, they may hibernate between November and April. During periods of warm weather, hedgehogs may become active for a brief time to search for food.

EUROPEAN

- Covered with about 5,000 quills that are cream colored, with black and brown speckles
- Each quill is about 1 inch (20 mm) long
- Gives birth to as many as 9 babies per litter
- Has a pointy **snout**, round eyes, and small ears that are mostly hidden by fur

EGYPTIAN

- Quills are banded with dark brown and white
- Has larger ears than most other hedgehogs
- Very good sense of hearing and smell
- About 5 to 11 inches (12 to 27 cm) long
- A fast runner
- Likes to burrow under bushes

In some parts of North America and Europe, it is illegal to keep European hedgehogs as house pets.

Hedgehog Highlights

Hedgehogs have existed for nearly 70 million years. They were one of the earliest **mammals** on Earth and lived alongside the dinosaurs. Today, hedgehogs are the oldest living insect-eating mammals. They are closely related to moles and shrews. In Europe, Asia, and Africa, wild hedgehogs live in nature. Long ago, they could also be found living in North America. They became extinct in North America about 10 million years ago. Hedgehogs that live in North America today were brought here as pets in the late 1980s and 1990s. Today, they popular exotic pets.

■ Humans have been observing hedgehogs fo nearly 3,000 years.

Hedgehogs have a very good sense of smell and hearing, but they cannot see well. They likely do not see colors, only black and white. They use stiff hairs, or "whiskers", around their mouth and nose to help them learn about their surroundings.

Hedgehogs use the quills on the back and sides of their body for protection. Hedgehog quills are not **barbed** like those of a porcupine. Unlike porcupines, hedgehogs cannot "throw" their quills at **predators**. Sometimes, a few quills can fall out, just like human hairs. The underside of the hedgehog's legs, face, stomach, and tail are covered with very soft shaggy fur.

■ Trying to force a hedgehog to uncurl may cause him harm. It is best to wait until he uncurls himself.

Fascinating Facts

- A hedgehog has a round body with a very short tail. The tail often is hard to see because it is so close to the body.
- Hedgehogs are nocturnal. This means they sleep during the day and are most active at night. Some hedgehogs can be trained to stay awake during part of the day and sleep at night.

Life Cycle

A pet hedgehog may live about three to seven years. With proper care, some hedgehogs can live even longer. A hedgehog has different needs at each stage of her life. At all stages, a hedgehog will depend on her owner for love and attention.

Newborn Hedgehog

Newborn hedgehogs are called hoglets. They weigh 0.4 to 0.7 ounces (12 to 18 grams). When hoglets are born, they are helpless. Their eyes and ears are closed. Hoglets depend on their mother for everything. She cleans her babies, keeps them warm, and protects them. Hoglets drink milk from their mother, too.

Adults

Hedgehogs are fully grown when they are six months old. Pet African pygmy hedgehogs weigh between 0.5 and 1.3 pounds (250 to 580 grams) when full grown. Other kinds of adult hedgehogs measure between 5 to 8 inches (12 to 20 centimeters) long.

Fascinating Facts

- Adult females are called sows.
- Adult males are called boars.
- Hoglets are born with quills. These quills lie just beneath their skin, so hoglets appear naked. The quills grow out quickly a few days after birth.

Weaning

At around four weeks of age, hoglets will begin to nibble at solid food. By seven or eight weeks, they are ready to be **weaned**. This means they can eat solid food and are able to take care of themselves. At this age, hoglets should be separated from their mother. Each one will need his own home. This will keep them from fighting with each other.

Quilling

Between 8 weeks and 6 months of age, young hedgehogs begin to shed their baby quills. They are replaced with adult quills. This may cause the young hedgehog's skin to become tender. He may ball up, hiss, and click at his owner. He may be grumpy, too. A hedgehog owner should handle the pet gently during this time. The new quills may take about a month to grow.

Picking Your Pet

Hedgehogs look like they are always smiling, so it is easy to see why they are popular pets. Still, hedgehogs are a big responsibility. Before you decide to buy one of these cute critters, ask yourself these questions.

Where Should I Buy a Hedgehog?

Most people buy hedgehogs from a pet store or **breeder**. It is a good idea to buy a hedgehog from a breeder. Most breeders work hard to raise healthy hedgehogs. Breeders can answer important questions you might have about your new pet, such as the age of the hedgehog. Make sure the pet store staff know a great deal about hedgehogs. They can help you select the right pet and answer questions about proper care.

In some areas it is illegal to keep hedgehogs as pets. Be sure to check the laws in your area before you buy a hedgehog.

■ Each hedgehog has its own personality. Some can be very playful. Others like to hide.

Which Hedgehog Should I Buy?

Both male and female hedgehogs make good pets. When choosing a hedgehog, it is important to be sure she is healthy and friendly. A healthy hedgehog will have bright, clear eyes, a clean moist nose, and clean, smooth ears. She should not have any loose quills or dry flaky skin. The hedgehog's nails should be trimmed, and she should walk without wobbling.

Before buying a hedgehog, you should also decide if you want her to be calm or playful. Be sure to handle more than one hedgehog so you can make the right choice for you.

Pet hedgehogs enjoy time outside of their cages to explore in safe areas.

Will I Be Able to Handle and Play with My Hedgehog?

Hedgehogs can be prickly. If you are afraid to touch or pick up a hedgehog, then it is not the right pet for you. When choosing a hedgehog, avoid buying one that will not unroll itself at the pet store. Be sure that it has been well handled so that it is not frightened by people. Otherwise, your new pet may be too scared to be comfortable with you. It is easier to train a young hedgehog to be handled.

Fascinating Facts

- A hedgehog can be adopted when she is about 7 or 8 weeks of age.
- It is normal for hoglets to make hissing sounds when you are nearby. However, if they make a clicking sound, they are angry.
- When a hedgehog hears a noise nearby, her quills will stand up in the direction of the sound. If the hedgehog's forehead quills are raised, she is startled or nervous. A hedgehog that feels safe and happy will keep all her quills flat.

Hedgehog Havens

A hedgehog needs plenty of room to move. One of the most important items you will need for your hedgehog is a large cage. The cage should have at least 1 square yard (1 square meter) of floor space. If the cage is made of wire, make sure the wires are no more than 0.6 inch (1.5 centimeters) apart. The floor of the cage should be solid to prevent foot or leg injuries. The cage should also have a lid to keep the hedgehog from climbing out. A large aquarium can be used for a cage if it has good **ventilation**. Place the cage in an area that is quiet during the day and away from direct sunlight. Give the hedgehog a hiding place, such as a shoebox with a hole cut in one side.

Some hedgehogs enjoy playing with a toilet paper roll. Cut a slit down the side of the tube so his head does not become stuck inside the tube.

■ Providing a large cage will allow a pet hedgehog to explore his surroundings.

Hedgehogs need a heavy food dish that cannot be tipped over. They also need a water bottle filled with fresh water daily. Rubber balls or sturdy plastic cars are great toys for hedgehogs to push around. Be sure to remove any parts that can be chewed off and swallowed. Hedgehogs also enjoy chewing on small rawhide toys.

Hedgehogs need plenty of exercise to stay healthy and happy. An exercise wheel is a good way for hedgehogs to keep fit. Be sure the wheel has a large open side and a solid or fine mesh running surface. A hedgehog can injure his foot or leg if the spaces in the wire are too wide. An 11-inch (28-cm) wheel is a good size.

■ Hedgehogs may enjoy playing with a variety of children's toys.

Fascinating Facts

- Some hedgehogs can be trained to use a litter box. Place a small shallow pan with dust-free cat litter in one corner of the cage.
- Hedgehogs need 1 to 2 inches (2.5 to 5 cm) of bedding on the bottom of their cage. Pine or aspen wood shavings work well. Cedar wood chips can cause health problems for some hedgehogs.

Mealtime Munchies

In nature, hedgehogs are insectivores. This means they mostly eat insects. Hedgehogs eat other small animals, such as snails, mice, frogs, worms, and grubs. They also will nibble on fallen fruit or other plant parts.

Be sure to feed your hedgehog dry crunchy food. Hedgehogs can have dental problems. Feeding them dry food will help to keep their teeth clean and healthy. It is possible to buy foods that are made just for hedgehogs. You can also feed your pet a good-quality dry cat or kitten food. It is important to feed a hedgehog once a day. She should be fed in the late afternoon or early evening, after she wakes up from her daytime sleep.

Hedgehogs often gain too much weight. A veterinarian can tell you if your hedgehog has been overeating. You may need to adjust your pet's diet.

■ Raisins make a nice treat for hedgehogs.

Fascinating Facts

- Pet hedgehogs should not be fed worms or other insects from the garden. They may contain germs, diseases, or chemicals that could harm your pet.
- Live mealworms and crickets can be bought at a pet store. They are a favorite treat for hedgehogs.

How much to feed your hedgehog depends on her activity. Begin by putting 2 or 3 tablespoons (30 or 44 milliliters) of dry food in the food dish. Remove whatever is remaining in the morning.

As a treat, hedgehogs enjoy bits of fruit, vegetables, or cooked meat. However, too much of these treats can cause an upset stomach. A hedgehog should be given these special foods in small amounts of about 0.2 teaspoon (1 milliliter). Offer treats three or four times a week. Leave the treats inside the cage for about 15 minutes. Then remove any leftovers.

Fresh water must be available at all times. Some hedgehogs enjoy a sip of lukewarm chicken broth as a special treat. However, they should not drink milk. Milk causes stomach upset.

■ Place water in a shallow dish. This allows hedgehogs to find and lap up water as they would in nature.

Tip to Toe

All hedgehogs have some **traits** in common. Whether it is an African pygmy hedgehog, a western European hedgehog, or a desert hedgehog from the Sahara, their physical characteristics are all similar. Some desert species have large ears and long legs. All hedgehogs have excellent hearing and smell. Some may walk in a slow waddle and some with short, quick steps. When danger is near, hedgehogs will crouch, hiss, raise their quills, and roll into a protective ball.

— **Hedgehog**

Furs covers the underside of hedgehogs.

Hedgehogs have a short, stocky body that is covered with thick quills, except on the underside, legs, face, and ears.

A hedgehog's face may be white-brown, or have a masked pattern. A hedgehog has a long snout with a pointed end. The nose is moist and hairless.

Hedgehogs' legs are thin and short. They have large feet with long, curved claws.

Hedgehog Housekeeping

Hedgehogs are clean animals. Most hedgehogs use their tongues to groom themselves. Sometimes a hedgehog will need some help getting clean. You can give your hedgehog a bath. Put him in a large plastic bowl or in the sink with about 1 inch (2.5 cm) of warm water. Gently pour some water over his back with a cup. Keep the water away from his ears and eyes. Use one or two drops of mild liquid soap that is made for small animals. A soft toothbrush or baby brush can be used to clean the quills. Rinse him well with fresh water. Wrap the hedgehog in a soft towel, and make sure he is dry.

Check your hedgehog's quills regularly to ensure that they are clean.

Keep your hedgehog healthy and happy by cleaning out his cage every day. Remove soiled bedding and droppings. Wash the food and water bottle well in soapy water. Be sure to rinse them well. Remember to put clean bedding inside the cage and to fill the water container with fresh water.

Your hedgehog's home will need a more thorough cleaning once a week. Remove all the old bedding, and scrub the cage with soap and water. You can use a **disinfectant** that is safe for animals. This will keep the cage free of germs that can make hedgehogs ill. Be sure the cage is rinsed well and completely dry before putting fresh shavings and bedding inside. Wash the hedgehog's plastic or wooden hiding place well. Cardboard toys should be replaced every two or three weeks.

■ Use products that are safe for animals when cleaning your pet's dishes, cage, and toys.

Fascinating Facts

• Sometimes hedgehogs foam at the mouth. They spread the foam over their quills. This is called self-anointing. Hedgehogs self-anoint when they smell something new or after licking a piece of wood. Baby hedgehogs begin to self-anoint as early as two weeks old.

Healthy and Happy

Hedgehogs can live long, healthy lives if they have proper care. However, like all animals, they can become ill or be injured. A hedgehog's spiny coat can hide some health problems. When handling your hedgehog, check her for signs of poor health. Some signs may be a change in appetite or activity. If your hedgehog is moving slower than usual or in a wobbly way, she may be too cold. Place the hedgehog under your shirt or on towels that have been warmed in a dryer. If you notice any other changes in your hedgehog's **behavior**, she should visit a veterinarian.

Some of the most common health problems for hedgehogs are skin disease and **mites**.

■ The St. Tiggywinkles Wildlife Hospital in Great Britain was opened in 1978 to care for hedgehogs that were injured by cars. Today, it is one of the world's largest wildlife hospitals.

Hedgehogs are very curious animals. They like to investigate anything new. Be very careful if you allow your hedgehog out of her cage to roam about the house. Keep your eyes on your pet at all times. An exploring hedgehog can break a leg, get lost, or become trapped under and behind furniture or in other small places. She may nibble on plants, cords, or other objects that may be harmful to hedgehogs. Some hedgehogs can climb well. They can be injured if they fall. Make sure your hedgehog does not climb too high and that she has a soft place to land if she falls.

■ A hedgehog's quills are filled with air chambers that can act as a cushion if a hedgehog falls from a high place.

Fascinating Facts

- Sometimes germs and diseases can be spread from animals to humans and from humans to animals. Always wash your hands before and after handling your pet or its food or litter.
- If you go on vacation, make sure you arrange to have someone reliable take care of your pet.

Hedgehog Harmony

When you bring your hedgehog home, he may be scared and upset. If he is curled up in a spiny ball, leave him alone until he can become used to his new home. After a while, you can hold out your hand for the hedgehog to smell. If you offer him a mealworm or a bit of food, he soon will learn that you are friendly. Sit on the floor beside the hedgehog or hold him in your lap. Let your new pet climb over and around you. Try not to make any sudden loud sounds or movements. This may startle your hedgehog. Talk to him softly and be patient.

Do not use gloves to pick up your hedgehog. Your pet should be able to recognize your scent.

■ If two hedgehogs begin making clicking sounds at one another, they are upset and should be separated.

Pet Peeves

Hedgehogs do not like:
- being startled when sleeping
- loud noises
- being handled or played with during the daytime
- being too hot or too cold

To hold your hedgehog, gently place both hands underneath his body. Support his whole body so he feels safe. Watch that your fingers do not get caught if he is startled and curls up. If this happens, keep calm and quiet. Holding a tasty treat, such as a mealworm, near his nose is usually the best way to make a hedgehog uncurl.

Some hedgehogs take longer than others to trust new people. Other hedgehogs may never enjoy being held. Still, it is important to play with your hedgehog for at least two hours every day.

■ Be patient with a new hedgehog and let him adjust to his new home.

Fascinating Facts

- To keep a pet hedgehog tame, he should be handled every day.
- Hedgehogs rarely shed hair or **dander**.

Hedgehogs and Humans

Hedgehogs have been around in legends and stories for thousands of years. In fact, Groundhog Day was once known as Hedgehog Day. It was first celebrated by the Ancient Romans during the Festival of Februa on February 2. People believed that if a hibernating hedgehog came out of her den and saw her shadow, there would be a clear moon and six more weeks of winter. European settlers continued this tradition when they came to North America. However, hedgehogs did not live in nature in the Americas. Settlers used another small mammal, the groundhog.

Some hedgehog owners name their pet Sonic, after a character in a video game, cartoons, and comic books.

■ Sonic the Hedgehog has appeared in more than 25 video games since 1991.

Fascinating Facts

• Tiggywinkles is an animal hospital in Great Britain. It is named after Beatrix Potter's hedgehog character. Each year, the hospital takes care of hundreds of hedgehogs until they can be safely released in nature.

Disney's movie version of *Alice in Wonderland* first aired in 1951.

The Tale of Mrs. Tiggy-Winkle by British author Beatrix Potter is a well-known children's book. In this story, a little girl visits Mrs. Tiggy-Winkle, a hedgehog washerwoman, who uses the girl's handkerchief to make clothing and other things for animals.

In Lewis Carroll's story *Alice in Wonderland*, a girl named Alice plays a strange game of croquet with the Queen of Hearts. During the game, rolled-up hedgehogs are used for croquet balls. The hedgehogs uncurl and walk away.

The Adventures of Hedley

Valerie Walker is a children's book writer and hedgehog owner. She has written *The Adventures of Hedley the Hedgehog* and other stories featuring Hedley, her pet African pygmy hedgehog.

"Hedley loves to explore. His adventures begin when a timid mouse named Marvin, joins him on his journey across the British countryside. On the way they meet a wise old hedgehog, rescue a young rabbit and narrowly escape being cooked in a poacher's pot. When they arrive at their new home, they barely have time to settle in before Hedley's nose leads them into new adventures."

Taken from www.hedleythehedgehog.com

Pet Puzzlers

What do you know about hedgehogs? If you can answer the following questions correctly, you may be ready to own a pet hedgehog.

Q Is it normal for a hedgehog to lose quills?

It is normal for an adult hedgehog to lose some quills. Hoglets lose their baby quills, which are replaced by adult quills. If a hedgehog loses too many quills, he should see a veterinarian.

Q What is self-anointing?

Self-anointing is the term used to describe how a hedgehog spreads foam from her mouth over her quills.

Q Should I give my hedgehog fruits and vegetables to eat?

It is okay to feed a hedgehog fruits and vegetables as a treat. Too much plant food can cause stomach problems.

Q How long do pet hedgehogs live?

Hedgehogs may live from 3 to 7 years. If they receive very good care and attention, they may live as long as 10 years.

Q How often should a hedgehog eat?

Hedgehogs should be fed at least once a day. Sometimes, they also can have a small treat or two.

Q What is the best way to pick up a hedgehog?

To hold a hedgehog, gently place both hands underneath his body. Support his whole body so he feels safe.

Q How often should a hedgehog's cage be cleaned?

A hedgehog's cage must be thoroughly cleaned at least once a week.

Hello Hedgehog

Before you buy your pet hedgehog, write down some hedgehog names that you like. Some may work better for a female hedgehog. Others may suit a male hedgehog. Here are just a few suggestions:

Needles

Snuffles

Pokey

Urchin

Thistle

Velcro

Tiggy

Spice

Pointer

Frequently Asked Questions

Should I get more than one hedgehog?

Hedgehogs live alone in nature. Once they are adults, they avoid other hedgehogs and will fight if they come nearby.

Can I let my hedgehog out of its cage to play?

A hedgehog needs plenty of exercise and new objects to explore in order to keep healthy and happy. It is important to keep your eyes on your active pet to prevent her from becoming injured or losing her around the house. Be careful not to step on the hedgehog.

Why does my young hedgehog sleep so much?

Baby hedgehogs, like other young animals, need plenty of rest. It is normal for a young hedgehog to sleep often when first brought home. Hedgehogs prefer to sleep during the day. They wake in the evening and are active for much of the night.

More Information

Animal Organizations

You can help hedgehogs stay healthy and happy by learning more about them. Many organizations are dedicated to teaching people how to care for and protect their pet pals. For more hedgehog information, write to the following organizations:

International Hedgehog Association
PO Box 1060
Divide, CO 80814

Humane Society of the United States
2100 L Street NW
Washington, DC 20037

Websites

To answer more of your hedgehog questions, go online and surf to the following websites:

Hedgehog Central
www.hedgehogcentral.com

Creature Features
www.nationalgeographic.com/kids/creature_feature/0202

Pets Hub
www.petshub.com/hedgehogs

Words to Know

barbed: to have a small, sharp point that sticks out in a different direction than the main point

behavior: a way of doing things or acting

breeder: someone who raises and sells animals

dander: flaky scales of skin, feathers, or fur

disinfectant: a special cleaning product that kills germs

hibernation: an inactive sleep-like state

mammals: warm-blooded animals with backbones and hair, whose young are fed with their mother's milk

mites: small bugs that live on an animal's skin or in its ears

nocturnal: most active at night

predators: animals that hunt and kill other animals for food

snout: the nose of an animal

species: a group of related animals

traits: distinct features of one's appearance or personality

ventilation: constant fresh air

veterinarian: animal doctor

weaned: beginning to eat solid food rather than drink a mother's milk

Index